P9-CBF-639

BKM
Guelph Public Library
JP FAN
Fan, Eric.
Night lunch
October 12, 2022
33281021246746

GROCERY

For Tara — E.F.

To Ellis and Ewyn — D.S.

Text copyright © 2022 by Eric Fan
Illustrations copyright © 2022 by Dena Seiferling

Tundra Books, an imprint of Tundra Book Group,
a division of Penguin Random House of Canada Limited

All rights reserved. The use of any part of this publication reproduced,
transmitted in any form or by any means, electronic, mechanical, photocopying,
recording, or otherwise, or stored in a retrieval system, without the prior written consent
of the publisher — or, in case of photocopying or other reprographic copying, a licence from
the Canadian Copyright Licensing Agency — is an infringement of the copyright law.

Library and Archives Canada Cataloguing in Publication

Title: Night lunch / Eric Fan ; illustrated by Dena Seiferling.
Names: Fan, Eric, author. | Seiferling, Dena, illustrator.
Identifiers: Canadiana (print) 20210353074 | Canadiana (ebook) 20210353082 |
ISBN 9780735270572 (hardcover) | ISBN 9780735270589 (EPUB)
Classification: LCC PS8611.A53 N54 2022 | DDC jC813/.6—dc23

Published simultaneously in the United States of America by
Tundra Books of Northern New York, an imprint of
Tundra Book Group, a division of
Penguin Random House of Canada Limited

Library of Congress Control Number: 2021949352

Edited by Tara Walker with assistance from Margot Blankier
Designed by John Martz
The artwork in this book was drawn and colored digitally.
The text was set in Harriet Text.

Printed in China

www.penguinrandomhouse.ca

1 2 3 4 5   26 25 24 23 22

tundra | Penguin
Random House
TUNDRA BOOKS

NIGHT LUNCH

WORDS BY Eric Fan

PICTURES BY Dena Seiferling

tundra

3 3281 02124 674 6

Clip clop, a midnight moon.

The night lunch cart rolls in.

Sweep sweep, dust and leaf.

Windows all aglow.

Drip drop, coffee's hot.

Noses sniff the air.

Shuffle yawn, bellies growl.

The night lunch bell is ringing.

Tick hum, oven's on.

Pots and spoons are clanging.

Hoot hoot, mince pie for Fox.

Badger wants a sandwich.

Crack crack, a dozen eggs —

sizzling in the pan.

One two, just like that —

sausages and peppers.

One two, just like that —

butter rolls and biscuits.

Rustle wrap, all to go —

puddings for little possums.

Sweep sweep, only crumbs to eat.

No pennies in the gutter.

Tick tock, time to stop.

The sky outside is brightening.

Here here, what have we here?

Little Mouse is trembling.

Sweep sweep, dust and leaf.

Windows all aglow.

One two, just like that —

a night lunch feast is waiting!

One two, just like that —

a night lunch feast for two.

Mouse says thank you, thank you twice.

Owl just nods and ruffles.

Clip clop, the morning sun.

The night lunch cart rolls on . . .